BINKY

BINKY

BY WILL BEALE

ILLUSTRATED BY VLADIMIR BOBRI

NEW YORK

LOTHROP, LEE & SHEPARD CO., INC.

To
STEVIE,
and
JIMMY,
and
TOMMY

BINKY

Binky gripped his home-made crutch closer beneath his arm and jumped over a drift log on his one good leg. He limped carefully around another—a smooth gray monster that some day, he told himself, he was going to clear—and kept hobbling as fast as he could go down to the beach.

Shelter Cove with its little white houses sprinkled along shore was even quieter than usual this morning, and almost deserted. It was odd, Binky thought, to see the empty fishing boats as they nibbled and tugged at their moorings, while the men, in their rough work clothes and rubber boots spangled with dried fish scales, stood idle and helpless. It was frightening, too.

Just now, most of the men were gathered around old Eben Seaforth, listening intently. Ancient, grizzled and weatherbeaten, old Eben was about the knowingest man of all the village. Sometimes he was sour and crabbed and grouty, and the men would call him "the old crab." But he knew about everything connected with the sea, and the men depended a lot on his wisdom.

Binky slipped in to stand beside him.

"Things is jest as bad all along the coast," old Eben was saying. "And I'm tellin' ye she looks woeful bad for this season." He gazed at the men, broodingly. "I remember other seasons in my time that opened up like this—not a herrin' in sight in all these seas, nor a line-fish. The canneries all along the coast closed down, the smokehouses empty—the people movin' away, or tryin' to starve it out stayin' behind."

One of the men looked toward the neat little shack standing at the edge of the woods at the far end of the village. "Hasn't the government feller any notions? How does he figger this thing out?"

"Ah, him!" Old Eben spat in contempt. "What can

he do, with his books and his phials and his miker-
scopes? They better keep all such as him down there
in Washington where they belong." Slowly the men
turned away.

Binky stayed. "Uncle Eben, does it still look bad?
Ain't there no sign of change?"

"No, lad. Scout boats have been up and down this
coast and not a big herrin', nor a little one for sardines,
can be found—not even with their new-fangled radar
contraptions for locatin' the schools. And all the big
fish—cod, haddock and pollock—will be leavin' these
shores, follerin' after the herrin'."

"Can't anyone *do* anything?"

"No man that lives, Binky lad. Now run along."

Binky turned and on a sudden resolution started for that little government shack at the end of the village.

Binky was a dreamer. Folks said he dreamed as much daytimes as nights. His lame leg prevented him from doing the work required of the other youngsters, and also from playing their games—the fleet-footed tag games, the races along shore, the swimming in the tide. So his chief entertainment was the make-believe adventures he had in the secret places of his mind.

Binky was an orphan. Someone said he had been born at sea; that his father had been commander of some big ship destroyed in the war, but Uncle Eben wouldn't talk about it.

When he felt like it, though, he would talk of other things—of fish and sea-creatures, strange and wonderful; of the great schools of herring that fed half the world—well, almost; he would tell of fishing for cod on the Grand Banks where the cod lived in millions; of Newfoundland and of seals and seal-hunting, tell of great whales—for Uncle Eben had cruised all over the seven seas. And he would tell of storms at sea, of gales and tides and currents—and once, he had told a thrilling tale of a whirlpool that had filled Binky with awe.

Binky had spent many hours dreaming of all these things, weaving them into make-believe stories. And in

4]

these stories, he was no longer lame, but raced and played and swam more swiftly than anyone else. Sometimes he made up his tales lying flat on the sand in a little secret niche, sometimes anchored near shore in the ramshackle old dory, staring up at the sky.

And then, last summer, Mr. Ames the government experiment man had come. Mr. Ames had been sent to the sardine section, from Washington, to experiment on certain feed which spoiled the herring for canning, and to impose inspections and regulations. Scoffed at and resented by the shore-folk, he was quite alone. Perhaps it was their aloneness that drew them together. Anyway, Binky had come to know him and to tag him everywhere — talking with him, learning from him, asking a million questions. It was Mr. Ames who first helped Binky to put his imagining into words —words that would some day turn into stories and sketches of undersea life.

And Mr. Ames, too, had talked to Binky endlessly, telling him things about the sea—but all from the angle of science—things that had never been known to the men of Shelter Cove. One of the most interesting things he told him was about the belt of herring and food fish that encircled the world, chiefly in the countries of the poor; he told him of their mysterious migrations, of the enemies that preyed upon them. He let Binky pore over

[5

his books, then he had sent out and got him more—everything he could find about the sea and its fish. Binky had *lived* with these books, so his dreams of the sea and its creatures had come to represent make-believe that was based on facts and so came close to the truth.

Leaving the beach, Binky clambered up the bank to the road, his anxiety urging him on. The road from the village seemed almost deserted, and he started furtively for the small shack at the farther end that served for a tiny experiment station. He moved stealthily, for Uncle Eben had told him to keep away from the Washington man.

The inside of the little place had always fascinated Binky. The microscope, the tiny retort, the unfamiliar implements made it seem like a mysterious grotto for solving the secrets of creation.

John Ames looked up. "Oh, hello, Binky!"

"Hello." Binky returned the greeting soberly. He had noticed the half-packed brief case of drawings and papers.

Mr. Ames was sober, too. "I'm leaving, Binky—to run down to Washington."

"You coming back?" Binky asked in a hollow voice. His friendship had come to border almost on worship.

"Don't know, son. I may come back soon—perhaps

never. You see, Binky, if the fish have left these shores for good, there's little for me to do here."

"But they can't have gone for good!" Binky said, his confidence unshaken. "Can't *you* find out what's happened, Mr. Ames? Can't *you* do something?"

John Ames shook his head. "I'm afraid not, Binky. No one can. The migration of food fishes has changed the history of more than one country in years gone by. Scientists claim that great mysterious changes in deep sea currents are what drive away the vast swarms of tiny feed. Or perhaps changes in the temperature of the water do it. No one really knows, Binky. Life began in the sea, and many of the great changes affecting the earth still begin there."

The boy dropped to the doorstep and sat staring out seaward. "But what do you think made 'em go?"

"We can't tell. As you've already learned, Binky, all creatures may leave their usual habitats for several reasons: because of natural changes, because their food supply gives out—sometimes because they are preyed upon by other creatures and are driven away."

"Do *you* think they're being driven away?"

"That seems most reasonable. But—sooner or later we'll know."

"How?"

"By keeping at it. By working it out in our own

[7

minds. Everything we have and are and know, Binky, has first been worked out in our minds. And, you know, seeing things clear in your mind awake is something like dreams in your sleep."

· Binky was tapping the floor with his crutch. "I've seen things awake, Mr. Ames, like you say." He hesitated. "Sometimes I get 'way off alone and make up stories in my head and imagine I can go wherever I want to—gee, I can travel myself *anywhere*—even to sea—and *in it*." He looked up, half apologetically, half sorrowfully. "When I get too lonesome I even go round the shore…to a place…and live with the fish."

Binky turned and looked through the door of the experiment station. Far out to sea, with the sun shining on their upper levels, lay soft gray mountain ranges of fog—shrouding the sea—keeping it hidden.

"Mr. Ames," Binky said, "it's going to be awful lonesome with you gone."

"Well, anyway, Binky, you can still make up your stories." Mr. Ames was encouraging as always. "Tell you what, you make up a really big one, and if I come back I'll help you with it. If you build it on all the sea things you've learned, it'll be a true story." He held out his hand, as to a man, and smiled into the wistful eyes of the boy. "Good-bye, Binky."

Solemnly Binky shook hands. "Good-bye, Mr. Ames."

[9

There came a day not long afterwards when Binky felt he could stand the loneliness and discouragement no longer.

For dinner Uncle Eben had salt pollock and potatoes with pork scraps; there were raw onions in vinegar for a relish, and for dessert there was a can of raspberry jam and bread from the store.

Binky did not eat. He couldn't. He was too filled with the trouble threatening Shelter Cove, and he was too unhappy about Mr. Ames' leaving. For days he had wanted to tell the men Mr. Ames' theory of the fish being driven away, but he had not dared. Mr. Ames had come to be associated with hard luck by every man in the village.

Uncle Eben was saying: "I'm plain spilin' for a fresh fish of some sort—a good mess of fried herrin', or a fresh haddick for a chowder." He pushed back his chair. "Grub's goin' to be scarce, boy. I thought I'd run along shore this afternoon, have a look into the sardine weirs, and mebbe ketch a fish or two, if I can dig up something for bait. Probably won't git much but it don't hurt to try."

Binky wasn't listening. Out of the silence he said: "Mr. Ames has gone away, p'raps for good."

Uncle Eben lit his pipe and disposed of the match with a snap of contempt. "Mighty good thing! That man has meant nothin' but trouble for the fishermen always. Fussed about sardines with a little red feed in 'em, and last year it was black specks on some of 'em—wouldn't allow 'em to be canned."

Binky persisted. "If only Mr. Ames had stayed, I bet he could find out what happened to the herrin'."

"He wouldn't know—no more'n a cat." Uncle Eben got up and began to pile the dishes together. "He better keep away from this shore for good. And I want you to forgit about him, you've got crazy notions enough as it is."

Binky's heart sank lower. He could say no more for a moment, and then he looked up. "Could I go with you this afternoon?"

"Yes. If you want to. There's nothin' to do ashore."

The boat was the usual small power boat for line-fishing. She was long and lean and sleek, and she was fast. Uncle Eben stood back aft, swaying easily with the tiller ropes. Binky crouched up in the bow, staring back at the receding shore. The houses of the village with their neat white fences grew smaller, and behind them ran the somber line of spruce woods, mounting darkly against the sky of brilliant blue. Farther up the shore stood the empty experiment shack. It hurt Binky to look at it.

They were picking up the easy swell. The sea pulsed

[11

and throbbed into long gentle rolls, gleaming blue and smooth, their rounded crests flashing in the sun.

Binky faced into it and was happy. The lift of the waves stirred him—the surge—the mysterious power he could never understand. *His* sea! He loved it!

There was no time for daydreaming. The boat turned toward shore, slipped past ledges and beaches, and now Uncle Eben was running in alongside a sardine weir, a great round trap of high poles woven with brush, standing at the edge of the tide.

The old man peered in through the brush. The water inside was still and empty. There was a deep loneliness about it somehow.

"Not a living thing there," said Uncle Eben. He pulled away from the great trap slowly. "Looks like main starvation to me," he muttered, and started the engine.

The boat headed out into the satiny blue rollers, out, out—on toward the adventure that, small in itself, was yet to lead to greatness.

Uncle Eben spoke: "We'll go out to The Deep-Hole off shore, Binky. If there's a fish in the whole Atlantic, it'll be out there. Might's well get the lines baited and ready."

Binky got out the wooden reels of cod line, with their stout hooks and heavy sinkers. Since not a single sardine was left for bait, they had dug some clams on the flats.

Uncle Eben anchored. They let out the lines.

For a long time there was nothing; the sea seemed empty.

Then Uncle Eben made a catch—a little brown-spotted tomcod, pathetic in its littleness above the endless sea.

Uncle Eben chuckled. "Now if *you* was a tomcod, Binky, you could settle about the herrin'—find out what's happened. This little codger's probably been huntin' 'em now—tryin' to find the rest of his folks that foller the herrin'." He threw it back.

Binky's mind caught at that. Uncle Eben was only joking of course, but supposing he *could* follow the trail of that tomcod—down there in the deep; could only . . .

A terrific jerk snapped Binky's line taut—almost yanked him overboard. He braced, and clung. The line swished viciously back and forth. Desperately he tried to hold it—this thing of the deep that fought him so fiercely. Slash, slash! went the line. Taut as a wire, it hummed and thrilled through his body. And it was dragging him down . . . bending his back . . . tearing at his arms.

"Uncle Eben!" he screamed. "Come quick!"

Down aft, Uncle Eben turned around, swept his own line around a cleat, and sprang. He seized Binky's line in powerful old hands, and held. A moment, and he pulled in, the line singing and thrumming through the water wickedly. Again he pulled in—fought and held—and again he pulled.

Binky watched, fascinated. All through his body he was feeling some mysterious unknown power, something he had never felt before. The boat seemed filled with it—and the day—and the sea around them.

Now, from down below, a furious gray form came writhing and fighting upward toward the surface—vicious, powerful, deadly.

Uncle Eben kept on dragging it up, his own arms yanked and slatted with the jerking power of it. Now the head came out of the water, long, gray, sharklike, with a pointed snout and a mouth well underneath set with cruel, snapping teeth.

"Stand away, boy!" Uncle Eben shouted. "Don't let it bite ye!" And he hauled another moment, panting with exertion.

Binky could see the writhing creature had a hide like gray sandpaper. It had powerful fins, and a slashing one-sided tail. But it was the eyes that frightened the boy most—clear green glittering fires, glaring up at them with terrifying intensity.

14]

"Blasted dogfish! Son of a shark!" panted Uncle Eben, hauling the thing up. "Haven't seen one o' them round here for years. Hand me that splittin' knife, boy, quick!"

Binky could hear it — the knife shearing sharply through the creature's neck. And he could see those baleful green eyes staring up at them even after the great gray body itself had dropped overboard.

Uncle Eben was sluicing a bucket of water along the gunnel of the boat to wash it off. "Might's well go home, boy. The fish have all gone, that's sure."

But Binky didn't hear. An idea had sprung suddenly into his mind, an idea so unexpected and strange it almost stopped his breath. Could it be these terrible dogfish that were driving the fish away from Shelter Cove? Could there be some great war going on undersea? He remembered some of the strange stories Mr. Ames had told him.

A few days later Binky was moving as swiftly as his crutches allowed him through the village, heading for the shore.

Ahead of him was a group of boys clustered around Sam Clukey. Sam was the know-it-all of the village, and now he was boasting as usual, evidently about going away from Shelter Cove. Sam was saying: "Course

16]

I've been down Portland way. And I've been way down to Boston. I've got a cousin there that's seen the President, too."

Binky did not join them. His mind was working hard at this other thing—how to keep people from leaving the village. He had an idea that might be the answer.

He had become almost certain that the herring had been *driven off the coast,* and it was these ferocious dogfish that had driven them. That terrible fish that Uncle Eben had caught had started him thinking, after Uncle Eben said: "This is the first dogfish I've seen around here in years."

Binky hobbled faster.

He was going to get away alone, where he could think quietly about the idea. He would take the dory and go round the shore to his secret place. There, where no one would disturb him, he could piece everything together, and then . . .

Someone was tagging him—fat little Gordie Smith, his sole playmate in all the village.

"Binky," Gordie pleaded, lonesomely. "Want me to play with you?"

"No, Gordie, not now.. I'm in a hurry. Got to go someplace."

He turned down the beach. Some of the older men

were talking, and he could hear dour old man Bassett saying as always: "Don't believe a word of it. Don't believe a word of it!"

In his secret place, Binky anchored the dory with a big rock, right above the stretch of bottom he knew so well. He lay back in the bow of the dory, his hands beneath his head, and stared up at the blue sky as he had done countless times before. He lay still, waiting for his thoughts to flow together, quieting his mind. He must rid it of other things to go down undersea to that snug little place on the bottom that had become so familiar to him—discover what was happening there. For today, he felt sure, he would get his answer—or at least be given some clue that might solve the problem of why the fish were leaving, and where they had gone.

"Let's see," thought Binky, and then—before he knew it, he was off again, making up another story.

And this time the story was going to be the greatest of all! He would put that little tomcod in it—follow him far undersea — and the terrible dogfish! Binky didn't know much about these small sharks called dogfish, but they'd have to come into it, of course. And all the other wonderful and exciting and mysterious things he had learned about the sea.

In this story the lone tomcod would be an orphan like himself; and he would have a crabbed old foster-father like Uncle Eben. There would be someone like Sam Clukey, bragging all the time, and perhaps someone like Gordie. And Mr. Ames . . . ? Binky's heart warmed as he thought of him. He would be the grandest character in his story—grand and wise as a king, or something—and he would overcome all obstacles and make everything end happily.

Far above him, in the intensely blue sky, the sea gulls were soaring and gliding through the air like flashing fragments of silver. While Binky watched, one wheeled abruptly and came dropping swiftly down on the inclines of the air—down, down, into the sea . . .

At the exact time that Binky was waching the gulls dropping down into the ocean, Tommy Cod, fanning his fins gently, poised himself in the water to look around at this lovely little sand-bottom in Shelter Cove.

Here and there through the clear green water the fish of the cove were feeding quietly—the smart young shore pollock watching for shrimp, the bright red perch from the Harbors of the Towns, the silvery young haddock, a wayfaring smelt. Down below Tommy, was the pale yellow sand, showing wavery shadow-ripples from the surface above, and around him were the homely old sculpins, and the lazy flat flounders. And here, too, was old Grandfather Lobster, and, more important, Grouty the Crab. Grouty, while no relation, had had a lot to do with Tommy's bringing up.

The last few days Grouty had been acting rather queer. He seemed crosser and crabbier than usual, as though he had something heavy on his mind.

Tommy flirted his tail impatiently, and swam around the rocks to the seaward side and looked out. Rising from the bottom, like tiny brown mountains, were hills and ledges covered with seaweed. Out beyond these, the water seemed thicker, and farther away, the sea was hazy and gray and unknown. Tommy had never been allowed to go outside of Shelter Cove, but often he was tempted to try it.

Now Tommy wriggled his shoulder fins restlessly. "I wonder what it's like, away out there. Why can't I go and see?" And that thought suggested another. "Why does everyone want to keep me here in Shelter Cove all the time? Who are my folks, and where are they? When a tommy cod is a year old, and ten or twelve inches long like I am, it's time he *was* someone."

He dropped down near the bottom where Grouty was scolding some mischievous little crabs scrambling heedlessly all about him. Grouty was peppery and cross at times, but he was the very wisest fish in all Shelter Cove, and he had always looked after Tommy Cod like a foster-father.

"Good morning, Grouty," said Tommy brightly.

Grouty grunted.

"Isn't it a lovely day?" Tommy persisted.

"If it's a lovely day, you want to make the most of it," Grouty snapped.

Tommy stopped. "Why, Grouty? What makes you say that?"

"Because this may be the last happy day you'll ever have in Shelter Cove. Now, run along—I don't want to be bothered."

Tommy laughed. "Pooh, Grouty, you're awful crabby this morning—must be sand in your joints. It *is* a lovely day. Shelter Cove is wonderful. And, as you say, I'm going to make the most of it."

"Where are you going?" Grouty asked sharply.

But Tommy swirled around to show his independence, and darted away.

Grouty watched him thoughtfully. Tommy was different-looking from the ordinary cod. His skin was dazzling white, and his spots and freckles were like

[23

pure shining gold. "Beginning to look like his father," said Grouty to himself. "And he's beginning to want to know things."

Tommy wound in and out among the rocks, trying to make up his mind what to do. Someone was tagging after him, slowly and uncertainly, as if not quite sure that Tommy would be glad to have him. Tommy turned, greeting him absent-mindedly.

"Oh, hello, Porgy."

"Hello, Tommy." The tagger sounded happy, as if relieved that he was welcome.

Porgy was a little round lumpfish. Like all lumpfish he was deep green and decorated with hard green lumps and little green warts. He was round and fat and slow, and Grouty the Crab allowed that he was a mite stupid. But he was gentle and kindly—he tagged Tommy everywhere, and Tommy loved him.

Tommy's high spirits came back. He cut a swift circle about his admiring playmate. "Want a game of tag, Porgy?" he asked.

"Oh, yes, Tommy!" Porgy said eagerly. "Yes, I do."

"All right. I'll beat you to that old lost anchor over there. If you touch it first, I'll catch you two shrimps and three sea-fleas—and this morning they're delicious." He poised himself steadily. "Now . . . ready? Go!"

24]

Tommy made a great show of swimming as fast as he could, but sometimes he let Porgy beat him, and this morning he let his little round playmate swim excitedly past him and touch the old rusty anchor first.

Tommy pretended to pant hard and be all out of breath. "Gee, Porgy—you're getting to be some racer!" he gasped.

And shyly, bashfully, Porgy wriggled his little green

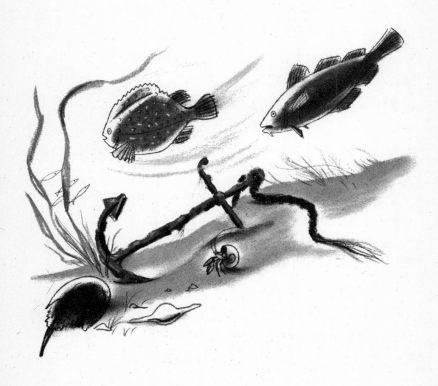

body off to one side, and tried hard not to appear so proud.

Tommy watched him affectionately. In a way there was something in common between them. Tommy had no family or relatives in Shelter Cove—that is, no near relatives. Neither had Porgy. Up to a few months ago Porgy had lived with a school of sardines, traveling with them all along the coast, safe and protected. Then one day the sardines were all trapped in a sardine weir along shore, and Porgy was alone.

Tommy turned way from his little playmate to look thoughtfully about the cove. He remembered what Grouty had said when he left that morning, and it bothered him. What *could* happen to Shelter Cove to make anyone unhappy? Maybe Porgy knew. He decided to find out. "Porgy—this morning Grouty said this might be the last happy day we'd ever see in Shelter Cove. What do you think he meant by it?"

Porgy pursed up his little sucker-like mouth and tried with all his might to think. "I—I don't know, Tommy."

"But what do you think?"

Porgy tried hard, and finally confessed: "I — I haven't got a head like yours, Tommy. My head can't think very good."

But suddenly Porgy began to remember. "I heard

Grouty talking to Grandfather Lobster this morning about..." He hesitated, trying hard to remember the words. "About in- invasions and—my-gracious—whatever he meant by that."

"Invasions and migrations," corrected Tommy. He pondered a minute. Invasions and such could only come from the far-off open sea. And if that were true—! A daring thought came to him.

He flipped about to face seaward. Perhaps out there he might learn something. "Porgy, let's swim all the way out toward the open sea! It's slack water now, and we can come back on the flood tide—be easier for you."

Porgy was terrified. "Oh, Tommy — I — I dassent. And I wish you wouldn't go out there either."

"Well, I'm going," said Tommy with determination. Then, a little doubtful about going alone, he added: "Are you afraid?"

Porgy's gentle little pop-eyes seemed sad over having Tommy leave him. "Yes, I am, Tommy," he admitted. "I'm awfully afraid." He stopped, and swallowed hard. "But if you want me to—I'll go."

Tommy was a good bit nervous himself, but he struck out, swimming boldly, and Porgy followed. But soon, as he swam ahead, with Porgy close behind, he forgot his fears in his excitement of the adventure.

There were so many things that were new. The

[27

passing fish were beginning to be bigger, some of them not at all friendly-looking, and Porgy kept close to Tommy. A big sea-pollock went racing by, and a group of huge tiger-backed mackerel. All were heading in from the open sea as if they were escaping from something.

Tommy swam out farther and farther, drawn irresistably toward the unknown world of the deep sea... dim, mysterious and full of danger.

Suddenly he stopped—poised tensely in the water. A group of fish, strange to Tommy, came toward them, swimming excitedly, as if seeking concealment.

Tommy plucked up his courage. He spoke to a scuttling little dollar-fish following the group. "Everyone seems to be hurrying. What's all the excitement about?"

"They say trouble is brewing out there," the dollar-fish said, and he scuttled away.

Tommy and Porgy stopped still. "Out there" meant the open sea. Close beside him Porgy said mournfully: "Please, Tommy—please let's go back! I don't like it here!"

"All right, Porgy," Tommy veered swiftly about and headed toward home, with the frightened Porgy, this time, almost outdistancing him.

Speeding along, Tommy said with determination: "Tonight I'm going to ask Grouty a few things. And while I'm at it, I'm going to ask about me. I'm going to make him tell me about me and about my folks. And I'm going to make him tell me what he meant about Shelter Cove."

It was evening and storytime. Down near the ocean's floor all was calm and still, and the fish-folk of Shelter Cove were gathered around Grouty just outside the hole in the rocks where he lived. There were the Harbor Pollock, the Flounder Family, Old Man Sculpin, and the Lamper Eels. At one side, three very young crabs were playing in a big pink empty scallop shell,

teetering up and down on its rim. Well up front, with the faithful Porgy right beside him, was Tommy Cod.

Grouty was the storyteller, and perhaps the teacher, too, of all Shelter Cove. He was proud of knowing so many things, and evenings like this when he felt like talking, all the fish-folk gathered around to listen.

Now Grouty began telling about his family, the crabs. He was saying, proudly: "In fact, some of my family grow to be twenty times as big as I am—some of them live part of the time out on land, and some of them even *climb trees*."

"I don't believe a word of it—don't believe a word of it!" came flatly from a bed of rockweed, and Old Man Sculpin turned his tail impolitely.

Tommy watched the little kiddy crabs dancing up and down on their scallop shell. He was thinking hard. All day he had been planning to ask Grouty what he had meant that morning about this being the last happy day at Shelter Cove. He plucked up his courage— now was his chance.

"Grouty, what were you saying this morning about Shelter Cove being in great danger? And what did you mean just now about enemies all around everywhere? We haven't got any enemies here in the cove, have we?"

"Not here, no."

"Well, then—why should we bother about them?

30]

Tell us, Grouty."

"Because—" But Grouty never finished his sentence, for at that moment something happened. All at once every fish in Shelter Cove began darting frantically here, there, and everywhere—vanishing swiftly out of sight.

Tommy Cod was alone.

He did not know why, but suddenly he was terribly afraid. Then his shoulder fins, back fins and tail began whizzing violently almost without his knowing it, and he, too, shot into some rockweed.

Just in time. Six or eight big gray strange-looking fish flashed into Shelter Cove from the outer sea. They were like small sharks, with long snouts and odd-looking tails, and their eyes gleamed green like sea-water in a bottle Tommy had once seen shining in the sun at the edge of the tide. They cruised all around searchingly, like enemy scouts looking for prey. But not a fish was in sight. Around the cove the powerful marauders swam, all in different directions, searching, searching everywhere. Soon they swirled about, came together in a band, and headed back toward the open sea.

Tommy, his heart beating wildly, peeked out from his hiding place and saw, far off, the great gray bandits heading along down coast like a plundering army.

[31

Tommy glanced around. Not another fish could he see in Shelter Cove, but down on the bottom Grouty Crab was squatting in front of the hole in the rocks where he lived, popping his black beady eyes in every direction, waving his horny arm-claws defiantly. Above him on a ledge lay Grandfather Lobster, his long feelers straight up in warlike defiance.

And now the fish were coming slowly out from their

hiding places, still nervous and anxious for reassurance.

Tommy Cod dropped down to the bottom.

"Grouty," he said in awe, "weren't you scared?"

"Not me. This old shell of mine wouldn't set very well on *any* fish's stomach."

"But, Grouty," said Tommy, bewildered. "What was it? What happened?"

"The dogfish have returned! That's what happened. They haven't been on this coast for years. And their coming back now means trouble—great trouble for us all." Grouty glanced concernedly over the little brood of young crabs.

"But why, Grouty? Tell me—"

"Dogfish are the bandits of all these seas," said Grouty. "They travel in packs. They kill and devour and destroy. They ruin whole coasts."

"But—do they kill all fish?"

"Chiefly they are the enemies of little young fish, and they're the great enemies of the herring."

Grouty was watching as all the fish gathered about him to listen.

"Herring are peaceful folk. Where the herring are, everyone is happy. But they haven't got much sense, and they travel in great schools like flocks of foolish sheep. One thing they do know. And that's dogfish.

[33

And when the dogfish show up from time to time, why, the herring and all their young herring-sardines just vanish from that part of the world and the other fish that amount to anything follow them. Where they go to, no one knows, not even shore-folk. If that happens around here, Shelter Cove will be ruined—dead."

The fish were moving about now, swimming restlessly, but listening to every word that Grouty spoke.

Tommy Cod cried out in protest. "But, Grouty— can't something be done?"

Grouty was slipping away into his hole. "Perhaps. If someone was smart enough, brave enough, and cared enough..."

"Oh, but, Grouty—don't *go!* Tell us more!"

Grouty's voice came back out of the dark hole, his words seemed to come from a long way off, and there was something about his voice that made Tommy listen.

"It might be a Tommy Cod who could change all this. It might be a Tommy Cod who could save all this shore . . . if he was smart enough, and brave enough, and cared enough!"

"Do you mean *me*, Grouty?"

There was no answer.

Tommy swam away slowly toward his own little hole in the rocks. Now the golden light was gone. It was quite dark.

Up in the world of light and sky and air, the wind was racing fiercely across Shelter Cove. Tearing over the surface, it blew the water before it in great long rollers, cold and gleaming and green, and topped with sizzling white foam.

Down near the bottom, though, aside from a gentle swaying, the water was calm and still. It had come on to blow pretty hard in the night, and the gale had driven a swarm of storm-tossed shrimp into the cove from outside. Up near the surface they were now scat-

[35

tered everywhere—tiny baby shrimp, with little pink bodies and black beadlike eyes, shooting through the water like traveling red sparks. All about, the fish were feeding peacefully, quite forgetful of their fright of the night before. Only the young Harbor Pollock seemed excited over the coming of the shrimp. They would keep their big round eyes looking toward the surface, would dart up with mouths wide open, seize a shrimp with a little victorious "plop," and wriggle swiftly back again.

Down on the bottom, Grouty had been cleaning the sand out of his house—sand and pebbles that the storm had washed in the night before. Grandfather Lobster came along slowly, and stopped to talk about that terrifying visit of the dogfish.

"It's those dogfish that's been keeping the herring away from our shores this season," said Grandfather Lobster.

Grouty was squatting on the bottom washing the sand out of his joints and claws. "I've been thinking that very same thing. With all these shrimp coming along shore, the herring should have been showing up long ago."

He looked through the water at a stranger who had come into the cove overnight and seemed to be listening to their conversation. He was a big pinkish fish with gleaming silvery sides. "I don't like the idea of the silver hake being round here," Grouty continued. "He's a rascal and a spy. And he's altogether too thick with the dogfish, always bringing his own crowd to clean up whatever they leave."

Grandfather agreed.

"I've been waiting to see what effect last night had on Tommy Cod," Grouty said. "Here he comes now."

He watched Tommy swimming along slowly, eating his breakfast on the way, but apparently without appetite. Tommy had hardly slept all night. He was still stirred up by the invasion of the dogfish the night before.

"That youngster has got the makin's of real stuff in him," Grouty said. "If I can only bring it out."

"He ought to have stuff in him," agreed Grandfather Lobster. "With the father he has."

"Yes," Grouty went on, "but he's still young and timid. "He doesn't realize…" Grouty broke off abruptly and cast a sour glance at the silver hake that had come near enough to listen. "With all this outside riff-raff showing up," he added pointedly, "I might as well begin on Tommy right now. Today."

Tommy had poised himself in the water nearby. "Grouty, what did you mean last night when you said I might be the one to save Shelter Cove?" He hesi-

[37

tated. "You see, I've been thinking about things. Who am I? Who are my folks, and where are they? Everyone round here has a lot of relatives but me." Tommy moved his fins nervously before he asked the great question. "Who is my father, Grouty? Where is he?"

There was silence for a moment. Not even a ripple could be heard throughout all the cove. Then Grouty looked straight into Tommy Cod's eyes and answered him solemnly.

"Your father is a fish of great importance. He is King Cod."

Everyone was still. The young crabs stopped their scuttling. Even Old Man Sculpin turned around to listen.

"He might be anywhere in all these seas. King Cod is one of the most powerful leaders in the ocean. With his great cod army he could drive every dogfish off to —off to the great unknown where the herring disappear." Grouty pretended to finish his cleaning. "There's no love lost between the cod-folk and the dogfish, and I wouldn't be surprised if King Cod might be willing to tackle it—even declare war—providin' he was asked by one of his own family connections, that is."

For a moment Tommy Cod was so still in the water he scarcely moved a fin. "Would he—? That is—do

38]

you think I could get him to help us? Oh, Grouty, do you really think he could save Shelter Cove?"

Grouty looked slyly at Grandfather Lobster. "I think he might, if you ever found him."

"But how? Where? Please, Grouty, tell me!"

"The son of a king must learn things himself— find his own way—make himself wise and brave and strong."

"But . . ."

Grouty was very serious now. "Well, Tommy, it's all up to you. And you must first get out into the big world of the sea. You must learn its moods, and its ways, and its dangers. And you've got to learn its folks— learn who their enemies are. And you're goin' to need help, but you've got to learn to pick 'em." Grouty moved away sideways on his legs, as crabs do. "I'd try Dusky Valley, if I were you. If King Cod should be on this coast, that's where you'll find him. It's sort of a cod outpost. Good luck, Tommy!" Grouty disappeared into his hole.

It was evening.

In the waters of Shelter Cove the light was fading. All the bright color of the day was gone—everything was soft purple shadows, with the fish stealing along like phantoms, and among them, unobserved, the stranger—Silver Hake.

All day Tommy had been swimming around by himself, thinking about the things Grouty Crab had told him. All day he had been wondering how he would be able to do what Grouty wanted him to do. How could one little tom-cod overcome the enemies of an entire coast? Now as he headed toward home he saw above him a fisherman rowing his boat in from the fishing grounds and looked up to watch the big shadow of the boat pass over his head. Every time the fisherman dipped his oars, the water around them turned to silver and gold, like liquid fire—almost blinding to look at.

From his threshold Grouty watched Tommy making ripples that flashed like silver in the dark. "You ought to see how you look now, Tommy," Grouty greeted him. "If you were as big as your father," he added slyly, "you'd light up this whole cove."

That settled it. All Tommy's uncertainty and indecision suddenly hardened into one big resolve. He spoke determinedly: "Tomorrow I'm going to find my father. I'm going to ask King Cod to come and save Shelter Cove." Then he swam off to his resting place.

A moment later Silver Hake slid from behind a big rock and, watching Tommy go, said to himself: "Tomorrow when you set out, young Master Cod, there'll be someone waiting to show you the way—to show you the way from which you'll never return."

Tommy Cod is going away!" piped the little crabs, scuttling around excitedly. And then they began chanting it:

"Tommy Cod is going away,
All alone he's going away—"

"I hear Tommy Cod is going away," mumbled a slow flat flounder.

"So it seems," replied his next-door neighbor. "They say he's going to find King Cod. Grouty's told him that King Cod might do something to save Shelter Cove."

[41

"Don't believe a word of it," advised Old Man Sculpin.

"Tommy Cod is going away,
All alone he's going away—"

The little crabs continued their shrill piping chant as Tommy Cod came around the rocks, pleased by his sudden importance. Nevertheless, he was nervous and uneasy, although he was trying hard not to show it. With a flirt of his tail he wheeled about and dropped down to the bottom where Grouty Crab squatted in front of his little house eating his breakfast. Grouty was holding a piece of fish in his claws, sucking away at it busily. Grouty's table manners weren't very good—he sucked quite loudly and he made bubbles when he ate.

"Good old Grouty," thought Tommy, with a homesick feeling at leaving him. But he tried to sound cheerful. "Well, good-bye. Thanks for being—for being so good to me." Though he wanted to, Tommy couldn't say anything more than that.

Grouty very deliberately sucked in all the scraps from about his mouth, wiped his claws in the sand, and replied crustily: "Good to you. Nonsense! You just remember what I've told you, that's all. Remember that you're a king's son, and live up to it." Then his harsh voice turned almost gentle. "And try to be careful and don't do anything foolish."

42]

"I'll try!"

Slowly, thoughtfully, Tommy stole away from Grouty's little house. He swam along shore to a small enclosure among the rocks that had been made into a playhouse. On the bottom and on little rock shelves were shells and colored pebbles; there were some bright sardine tins, gathered near shore, and even an old cast-off shore-baby's shoe that had been retrieved from the tide.

Porgy was there—in that little playhouse, lying si-

[43

lent and motionless in the water. When Tommy came in, he turned his back and moved away.

"Hello, Porgy," said Tommy.

No answer.

"Porgy," softly.

"What?"

"Aren't you going to say good-bye to me?"

Porgy flipped around in excitement. "I want to go with you," he blurted out.

"Oh, Porgy," Tommy said, "you can't. You can't swim fast enough! You'd get all tired out! You aren't big enough to take care of yourself."

"But I am," Porgy said doggedly. "Please let me, Tommy!"

"No, Porgy. Now listen. You stay here in Shelter Cove, and when I come back I'll tell you, oh—all about everything in the world—almost. And I'll bring you," Tommy hesitated, "I'll bring you something nice, something you'll like lots! Honest I will."

Porgy moved slowly into a corner of the rocks.

"Good-bye, Porgy," Tommy said.

Porgy replied with a very faint "Good-bye."

Tommy moved his fins with decision and rose well up in the water, up where he could see all about and lay his course. From down below he could hear the young crabs still chanting:

"Tommy Cod is going away,
All alone he's going away."

Tommy took one last look around Shelter Cove, then started toward the open sea. Beneath him, as he went along, the bottom of the ocean dropped down, down, strange and unfamiliar. The fish were strange, too, and the sea seemed so big and lonely that for just a moment Tommy was tempted to turn back, but he remembered Grouty.

"I'll find the way," he said aloud. "I'll learn about folks! I'll learn about the sea! A king's son must never be afraid!"

All at once he heard: "Good morning, Mr. Cod."

Mister Cod. That pleased Tommy enormously. Here was someone who evidently recognized that he was growing up, had already become of some importance. "Good morning," he replied cordially.

Silver Hake swam smoothly up alongside him—a handsome creature, with his pinky skin covered all along the sides with purest silver.

Tommy felt elated. In all the loneliness of the big sea it was good to have someone friendly to speak to. Grouty had said: "You'll need to know folks, but be careful how you pick 'em." But even Grouty couldn't find any fault with this splendid companion!

"Do you know," Silver Hake was saying, "you strike

me as being a rather remarkable young fish."

Tommy flipped his tail happily. "I do? Why?" he asked, anxious to hear more about himself.

"Well—finding you so far out from shore all alone. You must be very brave for one so young, and you have an air of fine birth."

Tommy started. So he was beginning to show it— his kingly parentage. He tried to speak modestly. "You are very observing, sir. My father is King Cod."

"Indeed!" in pleased surprise. "You see, I was right." Silver Hake swerved to one side in humble salute. "My respects, sir."

Tommy was overcome with importance. It was all going to be so easy after all—learning about folks, learning this world of the sea, conquering it. He could hardly wait to confide his mission to this wonderful new friend. "I am out to find my father," he said.

"Oh, really!" exclaimed Silver Hake. "Well, perhaps I can help you there."

"Would you know where he might be found—just at this time? They mentioned Dusky Valley. Do you know where that is?"

"But of course! You just follow me and I'll show you. It will be a great honor."

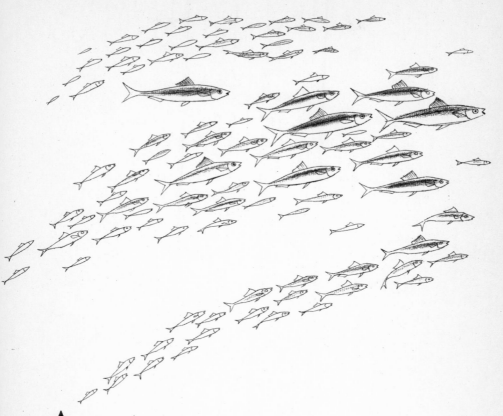

All afternoon Tommy followed his handsome
guide. He would never have dared to venture this far
out alone, even to seek his father. He was becoming
terribly tired. "Is it much farther?" he asked.

"Oh, no. Right ahead."

A moment later Tommy noticed a great swiftly moving mass. It looked like a gray-green cloud in the sea,
and it was streaming through the water just across his

path. Tommy swam closer, and saw that this moving mass was an enormous school of young herring-sardines, hundreds of thousands of them, all swimming straight forward, their backs showing almost black in the water, their bellies underneath gleaming like silver. Following closely after their leaders, they surged swiftly ahead, and not a single fish in the school was out of place.

Tommy Cod was astonished. He had not known there were so many fish in the world. Tommy swam toward them as fast as he could to see them more clearly before they all went by. It was like watching an endless army on the march.

"Where are all these sardines going?" Tommy asked.

"They're looking for feeding grounds nearer the coast," said Silver Hake, who was just behind him.

Tommy hardly heard, for suddenly a great commotion had boiled up in the sea, and terrified, the passing army of sardines began to break up and rush about crazily in every direction.

"What's the matter?" Tommy asked.

There was no answer. He looked behind. Silver Hake was speeding away like a shot. "That's the last of you, young Master Cod!" he called back.

Now Tommy knew what was happening. A band of long gray sharklike bodies, with gleaming green eyes,

48]

like the ones that had come into Shelter Cove that night, had shot in among the sardines, driving them apart.

Tommy Cod knew he had to get away. Working his fins and tail furiously, he swam faster than he had ever done in his life, the need to escape putting unexpected power into his fins. But even so he was not fast enough. He looked back and his heart almost stopped. Slasher, the leader dogfish, had left the others and was coming right after *him*. He was the biggest of these small sharks, and Tommy knew that if Slasher caught him, he was done for. He tried to dodge. He swam up—and down—like lightning, not knowing where he was going, losing all direction. Oh, how he wished he were back in Shelter Cove!

Now Slasher was almost upon him. Tommy Cod ducked and turned and flashed, but Slasher followed. Tommy darted up toward the surface. Right ahead he saw a great mass of wood and weeds, with clusters of rockweed hanging down below. If he could reach it, there was hope. But Slasher was almost upon him. Suddenly Tommy Cod whirled around and swam right under Slasher's belly, and before Slasher could stop and turn, Tommy had darted into an opening in that dark hanging seaweed and worked himself away in. There he stayed, almost motionless, with scarcely

[49

enough strength to move his gills to breathe.

After a few moments he peeked out. Slasher was circling around looking for him all along the seaweed. But he finally gave up and swam away.

Then Tommy slipped cautiously out of his hiding place. He had no idea where he was and he was too exhausted to sense his directions, as all fishes do. Dropping down, he could feel the tremendous pressure of the water on his body, but the water was still and silent and lifeless. Never before in all his life had he known a silence like this. For always, everywhere in the sea before, he had heard the noises of sea life—felt them: the swishing rush of nearby fins, the drumming thunder of distant motor boats, the sizzling of the currents about the rocks—the moving of the sea itself.

But now...nothing. He was all alone in the silent enveloping darkness.

Tommy was afraid. He swam ahead a little, but he was too afraid to keep on. He swam backwards a little, but that frightened him, too.

And then he remembered the important thing that had slipped away from him for a little while. He said to himself: "I am *not* afraid! I'm the son of a king. And kings don't—!"

He stopped.

Far ahead he could see a great black shape like a

huge shadow passing through the dim blackness of the sea. He knew it was some giant fish—for he could hear the surge of its great fins and tail, could feel the thunder of the displaced water through his own small body. Then he smelled a rank oily odor that almost made him sick, and he realized the great shadow off there in the darkness must be a whale. Whales had been in the sea off Shelter Cove looking for herring—all the fish had spoken of them.

Another huge shadow—off to one side. This time Tommy was too terrified to move. But again he stiffened his small body, and said aloud: "I'm *not* afraid. I'm the son of King Cod, and *he* wouldn't be afraid!"

With a little more courage he started to swim again and now that strange *feel* that guides fishes and birds through sea and air told him that he was going in the right direction. And faint as a whisper, he heard something...felt something...something familiar—something he knew.

Tommy dashed on again, his heart almost bursting, on toward that heartening sound that came throbbing through the water until he could feel it trembling through his own body.

The sea was losing its great depth and he could see more distinctly ahead. A number of fish passed him: sea pollock, haddock, a tuna like a barrel. He darted

52]

on. Again that sound—

"Di-i-ing! Do-o-o-ng!"

"It's a buoy bell!" cried Tommy. "A floating fog-bell like the ones on the ledges near the shore—like the ones near Shelter Cove! There must be a coast ahead!"

54]

When the first rays of dawn came down into the depths of the sea, Tommy swam up toward the light. Oh, how good it was! Good to be back near the shore again, where he could see below him the sandy bottom once more, and not far above, look up into the world of sun and sky and air.

He did not know just where he was, but thought he must be somewhere north of Shelter Cove. Already he had lost the feeling of "home," or home country; already he was thinking of the whole ocean as being his home. He swam nearer in to the land and looked about him. Here there were darting pink shrimps weaving trails through the water everywhere.

He wanted to linger, but he knew he must be getting about his business, and he swam off shore again, keeping north along the coast.

Suddenly, from behind, he heard someone singing:
"Come all ye little sailor lads,
    Come listen unto me.
  I'll tell you about a speakin' match
      For fishes in the sea—
  Up the anchor, crowd on sail
      Hold the compass steady;
  Call the watch from down below
      We're makin' down the eddy."

The singing stopped, and someone behind Tommy said: "Hello, youngster! Where do you think *you're* headin', out here all alone?"

There was something superior and cocksure about the voice, and Tommy looked back. It was a young cod —one of Tommy's own folks. He was older than Tommy and bigger. His brown spots were beginning to show along his sides like copper coins.

"Where you heading?" he asked Tommy again.

"I—I don't just know. I'm looking for someone who can tell me where to find King Cod. Grouty says our coast is in danger from the dogfish, and wants me to get King Cod to save us."

"Whew!" whistled Young Cod. "Who's Grouty?"

"Why, Grouty the Crab. He knows everything. He says the King can do it—if asked by a relation. I'm— I'm a relation."

Young Cod was looking him over curiously, noting the dazzling white skin and spots of gold. "So I see. Well, this looks to me like a chance for some real excitement, and I've always wanted an excuse to meet his kingship. Mind if I go along?"

"Oh, no. I'd like company. I'm looking for Dusky Valley. I've been told I might learn about the King there."

"Well," the young cod said importantly, "I think I

know just the fellow you're looking for—one of the King's scouts. The King has deputy scouts stationed almost everywhere to keep him posted on ocean affairs, invasions, and so forth. There's one in Dusky Valley, down beyond the Great Ledges. Come on. We'll look him up and look him over."

They started along, and Young Cod went on with his crazy little song about the speaking match for fishes of the sea:

"The star-fish reeled off all his lines
    Like actin' in a play;
The sea-cow said she'd like to moo
    But the sea-horse said: 'Neigh! Neigh!'
The tuna fish sang pretty tunes
    Of that there was no doubt—
But the whale walked off with every prize
    When he began to spout."

"Where are you from?" Tommy asked, when Young Cod stopped singing.

"Me? Oh, I hail from all over. I've just been cruising to the Grand Banks."

"What's the Grand Banks?" asked Tommy.

"Oh, ho! Ho, ho, ho! You a cod and don't know the Grand Banks! Heave ho, bullies, if that isn't funny!"

Tommy began to feel very ignorant. "I'm sorry," he said meekly.

[57

"Why, blimey, the Grand Banks is the cod heaven. It's a place off-shore where the bottom of the sea comes up to within a few fathoms of the top. The water there is full of feed, and all the cod—that is, all the *best* cod—go there to sport."

There was a silence, and then Tommy asked: "Did you ever see King Cod?"

"Well, shiver my timbers—*did* I? Why once on the Banks I was right on his starboard side—close as I am to you this minute."

"What does 'shiver my timbers' mean?"

"That's sailor talk."

Tommy liked Young Cod, but thought he was showing off.

They came to the Great Ledges rising up from the bottom in jagged, jumbled peaks and towers like strange black castles. Up, up they mounted almost to the surface of the water.

Suddenly Tommy shouted in amazement. Coming toward them from around the ledges was a round green fish, all lumps and warts, wiggling along like a fat little lump of hard green jelly.

"Porgy!"

Porgy wiggled up, looking guilty, but very, very glad.

"How'd you get here?" Tommy gasped.

"I've been in Dusky Valley lots of times with the

sardine school, so I knew about it," explained Porgy. "I thought I'd find you along here."

"Oh, Porgy, I'm so glad to see you, but you can't come with us," Tommy burst out. "You aren't big enough. Go back, now—go on!"

"I'm as big as you are," said Porgy doggedly.

"He means crosswise," grinned Young Cod, looking at Porgy's fat round body.

Tommy Cod tried again. "Listen, Porgy—*please* go back," he pleaded. "You might be killed. You might be..."

"No, sir, no, *sir!*" Porgy interrupted. "I'm goin' with you, Tommy, even if I do get killed."

He sounded so determined that Young Cod said: "Well, take him along—he's a stowaway and belongs in the brig—but we can't stay here all day."

Tommy looked at Porgy. "All right, then—but I hope you won't be sorry." They started on with Young Cod and Tommy in the lead, but after a while Tommy dropped behind and whispered anxiously: "Tired, Porgy?"

"No. No, I'm not." Porgy was too happy to be tired.

So they all swam along together, and it was a comfort to Tommy to have Porgy there, even though he knew that he shouldn't be.

Here we are, Chummy," said Young Cod, after they had been swimming for a while and were nearing a wide hollow that got deeper and deeper, with high hills on either side. "Your cod scout has his home port some-where down along," he told them. "Come on!"

With Porgy keeping pace, they hurried through the ocean valley that grew wider as it sloped deeper into the depths of the sea. On both sides the hills were covered with seaweed and rockweed, while in some

[61

places they saw strange sea-plants and sea-trees, green and gold in the light from above and changing suddenly to deeper tones of copper, brown and purple. They swam on down the valley and the water began to reach deeper and deeper.

Presently they slowed up. "We'll ask the way here," said Young Cod.

On one side of him Tommy saw a big cave. "What's that?" he asked.

"That must be the Grotto of the Squids," said Young Cod.

As he spoke, out from the darkness of the grotto darted one of the prettiest little fish Tommy had ever seen. Its long slim body was soft as velvet, and a beautiful shade of pink. In front of its head it carried a set of long pink feelers, all bunched together. Back of the feelers were big bright eyes, and—Tommy noticed a curious thing—out of its head, above the feelers, was a little pink tube, like a piece of pink macaroni. Sometimes, by squirting a stream of water from that tube, the fish was sent flying backward.

Young Cod watched it coldly, with something like contempt. "Odd-looking mess for a fish," he said.

"But isn't it pretty!" said Tommy, and watched delightedly as three or four others came darting from the grotto like flying pink arrows.

62]

Young Cod called to Tommy: "Come on. Let's pull our hook and get out of here!"

But Tommy lingered, fascinated, until suddenly the squids stopped playing and darted off to one side. Then he saw that an odd-looking object like a sinker, painted a brilliant red had appeared, hanging down into the water on a long string from above. The string began jerking it violently up and down, up and down, while the squids circled about excitedly.

Tommy had looked far above, where a dark shadow lay on the water, and he cried out to Young Cod: "That's a fisherman's boat up there. Grouty has told me all about it. That red thing they're swarming around is a squid jig, and he's fishing squid for bait!"

"We can't worry about them now. Let's go," said Young Cod heartlessly.

"No! No! We've got to save them!" Tommy plunged in among the swarming squids, crying fiercely: "Watch out for that jumping red sinker! It'll catch you! It'll catch you! There's a ring of steel hooks around it sharp as needles!"

Already Porgy was ahead of him, wiggling madly, separating the swarm into more confused groups. "Go back! Go back!" he cried. "Don't touch it!"

The squids fell back, frightened. In the confusion one or two of them whirled about, squirting a thick

[63

inky fluid out through their funny tubes, staining the water so it was impossible to see ahead. And in that heavy blinding cloud, Porgy swam too near the dancing squid-jig. One of the hooks caught him by the fin and pulled him swiftly upward.

"Tommy! Oh, Tommy!" Porgy called out helplessly.

Swift as lightning, Tommy darted into the inky cloud, groping his way. "I'm coming, Porgy! I'm coming!"

In a moment he shot up into clear water. "Porgy, where are you?" he called, but it was too late. The sharp hook on the squid jig had already caught Porgy and pulled him out of sight.

When he realized that Porgy was gone and would not come back, Tommy groped his way into the Grotto of the Squids and hid himself.

And there, Argo, the leader of the Squids found him.

"You must not feel too badly, Tommy Cod," he said, gently. "We all lose folks we love."

Tommy could not say anything, but he listened as Argo continued. "Sometime you may be a king. And a king must forget himself and his own troubles for the welfare of his people. Right now your own folk, your Shelter Cove is depending on you. So come along and we will help you. You have risked your life and lost your friend for us...and now it's our turn. Be-

[65

sides, the dogfish are our enemies, too."

Tommy followed him out of the grotto where Young Cod was waiting impatiently.

"Fall in line," said Argo. "The cod scout occupies a fortress just below. I'll show you." He led them down the valley a little space, left them and turned back.

Tommy and Young Cod kept on. Just ahead there rose a mound of smooth rocks with an entrance through a single twisted hole, and out of that hole came the great cod scout moving magnificently with easy strength and power.

"Good morning, young sirs—what can I do for you?"

Tommy had never known a cod could be so big.

"Please, sir," he began, "I'm trying to find King Cod."

"Why do you want him?" asked the mighty cod.

"If you please—the great schools of the sardine-herring have left our coast—the dogfish are driving them no one knows where. I have been sent to find King Cod to see if . . ."

"I understand," the scout said gravely. "I, too, know about the dogfish. We scout cod are stationed along the coasts to watch and report. I am about to report the invasion to King Cod myself." He was staring at Tommy curiously. "I can see why *you* were sent."

He stopped short and whirled about swiftly, his eyes blazing.

66]

While they had been talking, a long gray shape had stolen around the rocks like a stealthy shadow. It was a huge dogfish, bigger even than the scout, and its glaring green eyes were fixed upon them.

The scout could easily have vanished into the fortress, but scorning to run away, he whirled to face the enemy. Defiantly, quivering with hatred, he waited the attack.

Slowly, warily, the dogfish circled; slowly, steadily, the scout turned to face him. Like a flash the dogfish rushed. The scout leaped high and avoided him. Again there was a rush like a streak of gray lightning. Again the scout leaped, wheeled, and with a swift snap of his powerful jaws, tore a piece from the enemy's side.

This unexpected attack infuriated the dogfish. To seize anything in his jaws he had to run on his back. Now he shot forward upside down, jaws wide open.

Tommy watched, stiff with terror. He saw the two locked together, struggling and tearing. Unable to help the scout himself, he turned suddenly and rushed back toward the Grotto of the Squids.

"Oh!" he cried out to Argo, the leader. "Come and help—quick!" and he turned back, followed by the squid. It was pure instinct on Tommy's part—for the small pink fish speeding along behind him looked too helpless to do anything.

[67

The fight still waged, but it was plain that the scout was losing. He had already lost one of his shoulder fins, and was torn and battered from the struggle. But he still fought bravely. Then the dogfish drew back for a final charge.

Tommy was desperate. "Argo, can't you—can't...?"

With jaws wide, the dogfish was flying along on his back, straight toward the wounded scout. And then—Argo the Squid, rushed in front of that wicked plunging head, squirting his ink in a great black cloud as he went. The dogfish, blinded and confused, began trying to thrash his way out.

It was the scout's chance. The tail of the dogfish showed dimly in the inky blackness. The scout rushed in and his great jaws closed on that tail. He shook and tore until the big gray body of the dogfish, broken and limp, sank to the bottom of the sea.

The scout was badly hurt, but he ignored his wounds and moved painfully toward the rock fortress, with Tommy following. "You have shown bravery and wisdom, young Tommy Cod," he said with an effort. "You justify your royal birth."

"But how do you know who I am?" Tommy was pleased but mystified.

The answer came slowly for the scout was fast losing strength.

68]

"You have the mark of your sire on both your shoulders." He paused by the fortress to recover himself. "Listen," he commanded gravely. "The bands of the murdering dogfish are assembling, are sweeping on toward this coast. The dogfish I fought was sent to kill me so I could not go to warn King Cod." He paused. "I am unable to travel now. You, Tommy, must go in my place. You will find the King in the waters farther north. If not on the Grand Banks, then at the Cod Capital in the gulf. Take Argo with you. He is a brave squid—and he can guide you."

"Now, go. Find someone, if you can, who knows that north country—sea and land. Find the King and tell him I sent you. He will help you—he can and will defeat the dogfish. And now—farewell."

Tommy and Argo turned back up the valley. "Some fight, wasn't it?" a voice said cheerfully.

It was Young Cod.

*   *   *

The undersea world was fading, fading. . . .

A gentle bump of the dory brought Binky Seaworth to himself, and he stared blankly up into the empty blue sky. The dory had grounded on the beach. It was high water.

Binky caught up an oar and poled off, then started for Shelter Cove. That feeling of mystery pressed about him like a fog. And out of it came conviction equally mysterious. Now at last Binky knew the answer to the question puzzling the whole village. He knew for sure why the herring had left.

B inky pulled on the oars furiously.

Back in Shelter Cove he grounded the dory and hobbled up the beach.

He rounded the big half-buried log that still thwarted him, and hopped along till he reached a little group of the men standing over by the smoke-house.

"It's the dogfish," he announced, his voice ringing with conviction.

The men stared. "What dogfish? What you talking about?"

[73

"It's the dogfish that's driving the herring—driving 'em away, no one knows where."

Old Uncle Eben was standing farther up the beach and Binky limped toward him.

"It's the dogfish, Uncle Eben!" he repeated.

"Where you been all day?" asked Uncle Eben crossly. "I left your supper on the table. Go git it."

"But, Uncle Eben, it's the dogfish that are after the herring...honest, I *know* it! They get together in great big armies—to sweep the seas of every herring in sight."

Some of the men had gathered around, listening in amusement.

"Who's been talkin' dogfish to you?" old Eben asked with suspicion. "Where'd you git all this nonsense?"

Binky hesitated. To mention Mr. Ames would be disastrous. "I—I've read it—some of it," he faltered.

"Stop lyin', boy!" Uncle Eben told him sternly. "Or I'll take ye in hand. Ye sound like the government man."

"But—but—most of it I—I figured out in my own mind," Binky protested. "I just feel sure I'm right . . ."

One of the men laughed. "The guv'ment man's always been full of pipedreams like this."

Binky turned on him hotly. "Mr. Ames knows more'n anyone on all this coast! And don't you laugh —*Don't.*"

Someone spoke, drily. "I'm gettin' ready to move my

74]

folks and gear as far away from these shores as I can get. Didn't happen to find out what's goin' to come of it, did you, Binky?"

"No. No, I...I didn't," Binky admitted.

Another one of the men spoke up. "Couldn't tell us where'd be a good fishin' ground to locate, could you, kid? Couldn't make up something like that, could you?" And he laughed.

Binky blinked to hold back the tears.

"Binky, lad," said Uncle Eben more kindly. "Go home and git your supper, and try to forgit all this head-nonsense o'yourn."

Slowly, limping more than usual, Binky moved away.

In his bed under the eaves, Binky lay awake half the night. Next morning he went to the store for kerosene, and Mrs. Johnson, who was postmistress, gave him an envelope. "Here, dear—here's a letter just came in the mail boat. Says 'Mr. Binky Seaforth' —must be you."

Binky's heart almost stopped. The envelope was typewritten with his name—and up in the corner was printed: "From DEPARTMENT OF SEA AND SHORE FISHERIES, WASHINGTON, D. C."

Mr. Ames! It must be Mr. Ames—writing a letter

[75

to *him*. Binky was almost bursting with excitement and delight.

He got home as fast as he could and dropped the kerosene can inside the shed door. Then he hopped across the fields on a shortcut to the secret place on the shore. There, flat on the sand beneath the overhanging spruces, he opened the letter:

Dear Binky:

I felt I must write to tell you that our guess as to what had happened to the fish of your section appears to have been correct. It looks to some of us now that they are being driven away — as we suspected — by their oldtime enemies, the dogfish. Dogfish are being reported in great schools off the coast of Maine and beyond. There's been nothing like it before.

So the only thing that can happen to save the season down there this year is for the dogfish in turn to be driven off themselves—perhaps by *their* enemies, the cod—or by something we ourselves do not know. And by the way, strangely enough, the cod are showing up in those regions in great numbers also.

I hope this finds you well. Don't let discouragement get you.

Your good friend,
John Ames.

P. S. This would be a great idea for you to work into one of your stories.

Binky stared up at the sky, blinking the happy tears from his eyes. To think of it! Mr. Ames writing a letter to *him*.

Then he read the letter again. He read it four times.

And now that postscript had given him a great new idea; he was all alive with it. He was going to the undersea world again—this time to deeper depths— and work it all out in his imagination. And this time he might really find the answer that even Mr. Ames and the men in Washington were unable to figure out. He, Binky, might be the one to discover the way to defeat the dogfish.

He folded the letter carefully—put it inside his shirt, and hopped back across the fields.

His mind was already churning with questions. Who could possibly overcome the dogfish...who in all the deep? Would it be the cod? He thought that was what Mr. Ames had hinted.

"If I can only figure out how Tom Cod and Argo and Young Cod made out—" he said to himself.

But for days there was no opportunity. A big storm from off the sea filled all Shelter Cove, and Binky had to stay indoors with Uncle Eben. And with Uncle

78]

Eben there with him he could not concentrate. The only place he could think, it seemed, was in his dory, looking deep, deep down into the sea.

And then fair weather broke. Next morning Uncle Eben's dory was anchored again, at the edge of the tide. The fog lay off outside the cove, the sun shining on its upper margin like soft white wool. But fog would not prevent Binky from going out and getting around to the secret place.

Down on the beach Binky hobbled into Uncle Eben's fish stand. He gathered up a warm pea-jacket of the old man's, another coil of line, then climbed into the dory and rowed around the point. There, in the tiny inlet he anchored the dory and sat a minute, resting. Rocking gently in the boat, the pea-jacket warm about him, Binky settled down, and stared intently into the fog that was drifting thinly across the cove.

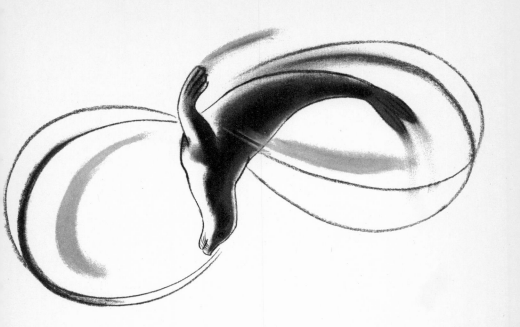

Hurry-hurry-hurry!

Hurry, hurry, hurry, hurry!

All day the three dispatch messengers shot along
the coast—never halting, never lingering.

They came upon some big sea-pollock, playing along
after shrimp, all fed to fatness, with big sagging bellies.

"How far to the Grand Banks?"

"A hundred leagues—then keep off shore."

They shot by coves and inlets, skirted long capes
and headlands jutting out to sea. They crossed wide
bays.

[81

"How far to the Grand Banks?" they asked a group of haddock.

"Fifty leagues! When you sight the Scattered Islands, strike out to sea." As the haddock sped by they called back: "The fleet's on the Grand Banks just now. Look out for yourselves!"

Late in the day, Young Cod began to complain discontentedly. "Marlin spikes and deadeyes—my fins are numb and my tail feels like an unshipped rudder! We've got to make port and come to anchor for the night. I'm about ready for Davy Jones Locker, making such a headlong cruise as this."

Tommy himself was so tired that he felt he couldn't swim another league. But already his experiences were hardening him, already he was losing some of his fear of things, was beginning to know his own strength and courage.

He looked at Argo patiently swimming beside him. All day the squid had been silent, his tentacles bunched close together in front of him, like a tight bundle of pink pencils tapering to a point. Argo could outswim either of them when he wanted to. But he did not have so much endurance, and occasionally he would flirt his body around, and squirting a steady stream of water out of his ink-tube, would shoot along backward just to rest himself.

Now Argo looked tired. "I think it wise to rest for the night," he told Tommy. "We'll all make better progress tomorrow."

They turned aside, swam in from the sea, and found a sheltered cove deep in among the headlands. It was a peaceful place. There was a sandy bottom with seaweed-covered rocks, and the fish were all familiar.

Up in the world of light and sky and air, the sun was going down in green and yellow glory. The water was alive with shrimp, and the three messengers began to feed ravenously.

All day Tommy had been thinking of how the scout had told him to find someone who knew the north country, *sea and land*. Perhaps in this very cove he might meet someone who answered that description.

Suddenly from above him, a seal came cruising through the clear green water, doing all sorts of things on the way—nose-diving, turning somersaults, rolling over and over, doing flip-flaps and figure eights, enjoying himself immensely.

It made Tommy think of the first time he had ever seen one of the seal-folk down coast in the home-country. Questioned about it, Grouty had said to Tommy: "That was a seal, and *there's* a critter that knows sea and land."

[83

Remembering this made Tommy so excited he forgot to eat. "Good evening, Mr. Seal," he said eagerly.

"The name's Ho-Happy," said the seal. And he straightened up, bent over frontwards, and rolled completely under himself.

"I'm very glad to make your acquaintance," said Tommy politely. And he added: "Just now, I'm specially glad."

Ho-Happy stood up straight on his tail-flippers and spun around twice. "What's on your mind?"

"Invasions and migrations," said Tommy importantly.

"Whose and what?"

"Dogfish and herring," said Tommy, and told him what had happened.

"Oh, so that's it." Ho-Happy was studying a scrap of seaweed in a front flipper. "Well, Your Young Highness," he said, "I've been hearing all about this. It so happens that the dogfish are no friends of the seal-folk either. If the herring are driven away, we seals will have to be on the move also."

Tommy flipped his tail excitedly, pleased at being recognized as the King's son. "Is it true," he asked eagerly, "that you know sea *and* land?"

"So I'm told."

"And you can look out over both and tell what's

going on?"

"Guesso."

"And you know all the north country?"

"Oughto."

"Will you come with us and help us?"

Ho-Happy darted away on a wide arc, and then came rushing back.

"I've thought it all over," he said with an air of great consideration though he had been gone only a few seconds, "and I may as well go with you. You'd better fill your royal poke with grub, Your Young Highness, and we'll strike out in the morning. You've got a hard trip ahead of you."

The very first day he was with them Ho-Happy showed his worth as a guide. As they came in sight of the Scattered Islands, he slowed up and announced: "I'm going aloft for a breath of air and get my bearings."

A few moments later he dropped down again. "Just as I thought," he said. "Up ahead is Lost Ship Reach, running swift between the shore and Great Island. If we'd kept on, we'd have run straight into the Old Sow."

"What's the Old Sow?" asked Tommy.

"It's a place where a big island splits the tides. They

come roaring together at the other end, forming the Old Sow, one of the greatest whirlpools in the world. Some call it 'Old Spinner.' Come on, I'll show you. But don't go too near."

"I guess I'll stay here." Young Cod grinned. "I'm not particularly interested in scenery."

But Tommy was fascinated and went closer, to the very edge of the whirlpool. He was so interested he did not notice that his small body was being pulled slowly along, closer and closer to that whirling tunnel, spinning and roaring deep down in the sea. The round whirling sides, smooth and gleaming, spun so fast that it dazed him to watch and he felt himself being dragged slowly and surely into the dreadful cone. Then, just in time, Ho-Happy the Seal swam toward him with his powerful strokes and forced him back.

"That was a close call!" he exclaimed when Tommy was safely back in still water.

"I didn't know a whirlpool pulled so hard!" Tommy gasped. Later he would remember his escape.

At noon they paused to feed. Then, their meal finished, Ho-Happy swung into action, with Tommy beside him and Young Cod and Argo, the Squid, swimming behind.

Again Tommy Cod asked the question that was so important to him. "Have you ever seen King Cod?"

[88

Ho-Happy looked at him soberly. "Yes, I've seen him. He is a wonderful king."

Tommy was silent. All at once other things attracted his attention. Signs of unrest appeared among the fish. The ones they passed were keeping close to the shore, scattering among the rocks and ledges, as though looking for places to hide.

Tommy swung about to question a lumbering old hake. He was lank and thin, with a big head and sagging belly. "What's happening?" Tommy inquired.

"News from outside."

"What do you mean?"

"The greatest school of sardine-herring in years is outside, being kept away from these coasts." He looked about, gloomily. "I'm old and I've seen a lot, but I never knew the like of *this* school. And all out to sea behind this big army of herring, the dogfish are assembling their forces—dogfish, and their camp-followers, the silver hake."

"What do you think'll happen?"

"Invasion. Invasion like we've never seen. If the dogfish succeed in driving *this* school to all points of the compass, the herring'll probably vanish off these coasts as they've done before, and you'll see hard times in this part of the world—very hard times!"

"We must hurry," said Argo.

[89

"Hurry," echoed Young Cod.

They left the region of the Scattered Islands, rising bold and steep from the bottom, and swung out to sea.

It was then they saw the first signs of the invasion the old hake had mentioned. Small schools of sardine-herring were moving about uncertainly, not knowing which way to turn.

Ho-Happy spoke. "Guess the big school's getting scared all right. These fugitives are all mixed up. Let's make the Grand Banks and find the King. There's no time to lose."

Just ahead of the dispatch-messengers lay the great undersea plains of the Grand Banks, a region where the bottom of the sea rose up to a wide plateau. It was here on the sandy plains nearer the surface that the cod roved, thousands and thousands of them, great and small.

Tommy Cod, fascinated, watched them traveling here, there and everywhere, winding, turning, wandering; he gazed at the ships above, their round bottoms familiar—he saw the cod-trawls hanging in the water close by, and others anchored far off in every direction. All this was part of his education.

Suddenly Young Cod cried out: "Well, blow me down! Off there is one of our scouts!"

"Let's talk to him!" Tommy exclaimed. "Come on!"

The scout was a big fish like the one they had left behind in Dusky Valley, and they could tell he was a scout by his dark brown spots, almost purple against his tawny, freckled skin. They swam eagerly toward him.

"We've been sent by the Dusky Valley scout to see King Cod," Tommy said.

"What was his message?" The big fish eyed him gravely.

"The invasion of the dogfish. It seems right at hand."

"Yes. We've been expecting it. But the King is not on the Banks. He's at the Cod Capital in the gulf. Get to him, quickly as you can—we can't leave here. Tell him your message." He glanced up at little splattered spots here and there on the surface of the ocean—sea-birds dipping their heads and necks swiftly up and down. "The gulls are washing and oiling themselves. The fishermen say that when they do that, it's a sign of a great storm. So hurry—get across the gulf as soon as you can. It's coming a no'theast gale, and the gulf will be difficult."

Ho-Happy had darted up to the surface, then dropped down again. "The fleet is calling home all the dories—must be looking for a whale of a gale. Get your sea-legs on, you're goin' to need 'em."

[91

Tommy Cod had never seen a storm at sea before. In Shelter Cove there had been rainstorms and squalls, and small scraps of gales, but he had never dreamed of the fury that could boil up on the open sea, with all the winds of the upper world raging and screaming, and the ocean rocked and shaken to its very depths.

Tommy never forgot that storm. It made him feel some strange and mysterious power, bigger and

[93

stronger than all the Tommy Cods in the world, bigger and stronger than whales, bigger than shore folk, bigger even than kings.

As they traveled toward the gulf, the sea above grew darker, and they noticed the fish leaving the upper levels, seeking the safety of the depths. Double anchors came hurtling down to the bottom from the fishing ships far above, making white streaks through the water before they dove into the mud. And all the little dark spots above them that had been dories scuttled back to their mother-ships, and then vanished right up out of the water.

It began to hail.

Tommy Cod had never seen hail. "Oh, look!" he cried, rising up toward the surface. "Isn't it pretty?"

The ocean was being pelted with millions of little white balls that struck and bounced and then disappeared, leaving little circles that merged and vanished into each other.

Moving swiftly, with powerful strokes, Ho-Happy joined Tommy. "Yes, it's pretty, all right. But it's hail, and that's frozen rain. And it means cold winds and big trouble. Let's go."

As they sped along, it grew almost black in the sea. The upper world of water was wild and fearful, forming into huge brown hollows that swelled up into towering hillocks that turned green and then burst into writhing, hissing foam and covered all the sea.

"The squall has struck!" said Young Cod. "It's beginning to blow hard. Gales in this gulf are the worst in the world."

Ho-Happy said: "I'm going up for a whiff of air."

Tommy looked at the others. Young Cod swayed along, confident of himself. Beside him Argo the Squid swam steadily.

In a little while Ho-Happy came back. "Going to be a rip-tail snorter. Looks pretty bad all right!"

By now they had left the broad high plains of the Grand Banks and were approaching the deeper waters of the gulf.

Tommy began swimming up, where it was lighter.

"Be careful!" Ho-Happy shouted. "Keep down till we strike the gulf!" And in a second, "Look out! A giant wave!" he cried.

Too late. Tommy, as though he were a tiny chip, was swept up to the surface and hurled through the air, fluttering and gasping, far across the foam. Then Tommy felt the full impact of the world of winds and waves and darkness, of toppling seas and screaming winds.

"Plop!"

Tommy was down again, gasping for the breath

that he could not get up in the air. Argo swam quickly toward him.

"We've been back there searching for you," he said.

Young Cod joined them from somewhere in the dimness. "That was a close call, youngster," he remarked. "But you'll learn."

"Glad you're back, Tommy," Ho-Happy said soberly. And Tommy, still shaken, swam close to Ho-Happy's side.

Now they were in the gulf itself, and the sea, deeper here, stirred and swayed and rocked mightily.

"We'll have to drop to where there's not so much motion," said the seal, and they slanted down, where, just visible in the dim light, were black gloomy mountains and valleys, running ever deeper and deeper.

When at last they met a cod scout, Tommy could have shouted for joy.

"Which way to the Cod Capital?" they all cried out at once.

And the scout called back: "Straight ahead."

"Is King Cod there?"

"Yes. At the Royal Grotto. Anyone'll show you! Some storm!"

On they sped, with renewed courage.

Next they met a platoon of cod, a scout leading them.

96]

"Where's the Royal Grotto?" they asked.

"Turn in between two towering islands. Tell your errand to the guards."

The sea was calmer now. And on all sides full-grown cod were coming and going as if on urgent business.

The two islands rose upright like pillars in the sea near the coast that showed dimly ahead. At the entrance two guards asked them their business.

Tommy explained eagerly. "We've come to ask the King's help. We've brought a message from the Dusky Valley scout."

The guards were studying him intently as he spoke, taking note of his dazzling white skin with the gold spots on his shoulders.

"Enter, Your Highness!"

The entrance led through water, still and wonderfully clear, to a great undersea cavern where important-looking cod came and went continuously.

Farther in, a brisk young lackey-cod met them. "Follow me," he said, and led the way through a guarded passage into a lofty grotto, open to the surface. Light was coming from above, and gleamed all around them, revealing the undersea splendor of rough jagged walls towering up through the clear amber water. The walls were deep somber purple, turning to

[97

dusky sable in the shadows. The floor of the grotto it-self was rock-strewn sand. At the far end they saw a smaller niche in the bronze-colored walls. And there, on his deep sea throne, they found King Cod.

Tommy was completely dazzled by his first glimpse
of the King. From head to tail he seemed a creature of
living gold. His pale freckles and tawny spots all melted
together, and with every movement he flashed and glit-
tered like polished metal.

The King looked at his four visitors with a kindly
curiosity, his eyes going over small Tommy with sudden interest. "You have something to say to me, my
son?" he questioned.

"My son!" As he heard these words, Tommy Cod was filled with a happiness and pride and worship almost too great to bear.

He got his breath at last. "If you please, Your Majesty," he began, "we have come to seek your help."

"Yes. Go on."

"It's about Shelter Cove."

"Shelter Cove? That's far down the coast, is it not?"

"Yes, sir—I mean, Your Majesty."

"Down below Spinner, the great whirlpool?"

"Yes, Your Majesty." Tommy started to ask how he knew, and then remembered that it was a king's duty to know everything. "The herring schools are off shore," he continued, "in numbers like never before. They mean food—and life to Shelter Cove and all our shore. But the dogfish are getting ready for an invasion, to break them up and drive them no one knows where— drive them away, perhaps for good."

The King's gleaming body and shining fins moved restlessly. And now Tommy saw what he had not noticed before—the scars and marks of old warfare on the flashing golden skin.

"Yes, I know," the King was saying in his grave, kindly voice. "For some time I have been aware of it. Our scouts have already been reporting to us. But first —who sent you to me, my son?"

100]

"Grouty the Crab sent me. Do you know Grouty?"

"Not personally. But I know his family—an ancient one, and wise."

The King summoned some of his attendants, spoke to them crisply, and they darted away to obey his command. He turned back to look at Young Cod, at Argo, and Ho-Happy the Seal. "And these friends of yours, are they willing to help?"

"Oh, yes, Your Majesty!" they all answered at once.

"Well then, there is no time to lose." The King had laid aside his gentle fatherly manner—had become a Sovereign, firm and austere.

Turning, he beckoned to Young Cod. "You, Young Cod—come here beside me and listen carefully."

And Young Cod, his manner no longer impudent, obeyed. He listened intently, and departed at once.

Then Argo the Squid. Argo's orders were evidently long and complicated. Finally he saluted with all his pink tentacles and withdrew. Passing Tommy, he whispered: "Good-bye, Tommy. In the saving of Shelter Cove...I'll be there," and he shot toward the entrance.

Ho-Happy had excused himself a moment before and darted upward to the great opening in the ceiling for a breath of air from the surface of the outside sea world. Now he had dropped down again, refreshed and strong, and ready for his own mission.

[101

"Ho-Happy," said the King gravely. "Your seal-folk and my cod subjects have always lived together in these northern seas, peaceably and for our mutual welfare. I want you to go quickly to your seal-folk— tell them I need their help. Our enemies, the dog-fish, have been their enemies also. This is what I want them to do." And he counseled Ho-Happy gravely.

Again Ho-Happy shot straight upward through the water of the audience hall. Only his swift-moving shadow traveled the golden sand below. Up he went, up to that opening above, and then disappeared, his shadow with him.

The king called a passing cod. "See that Tommy is fed and rested and made ready for the foray. Let no ill befall him, for Tommy goes with me."

Tommy followed the attendant out. They moved easily through undersea corridors into a courtyard where the sun of the upper world shone down clearly, lighting the hard sand, the white rocks and the sea plants that were growing everywhere.

Tommy fed on mollusks, on delicious fish-eggs, and on some peculiar sea-worms that he had never seen in the days of Shelter Cove.

"Shelter Cove," he thought. "How far away it seems."

He thought of Grouty the Crab. He wondered what they were all doing—Grouty, Grandfather Lobster, the flounders and sculpins, Rose Red, the perch. Then he

102]

thought with loneliness and sorrow of little fat Porgy.

"I wonder if I shall ever see Shelter Cove again," Tommy said to himself.

The war was on.

From all over the kingdom, cod were assembling swiftly. In great hosts they were gathering — from every corner of the gulf, and from the farthest outposts beyond. In companies they came, big trained warriors, sleek and swift and strong. In rough-looking bands they came, from the wild region farther north — odd-looking fighters these, with darker battle-scarred skins, fierce and wild in their appearance. And they were greeted with cheers.

And last of all, out from his undersea grotto, came the King, in all his golden glory, and beside him, bearing himself proudly, was Tommy Cod.

At their appearance, the armies settled to stillness, poised and barely moving in the gentle sway of the currents. There was deep silence.

Then the King spoke. "Our ancient enemies, the dogfish, are invading our coasts to the south. They are attacking the herring, driving them, scattering them —destroying them.

"But we are marching on these enemies, my soldiers. We are the greatest army in all the world of the ocean!" He was interrupted here by a long outburst of cheers. "With your help we will drive these invaders from our seas—drive them, conquer them, destroy them! March on!"

Again that great tumult of acclaim. Then, led by King Cod, with Tommy Cod close beside him, the cavalcade streamed forth from all the thoroughfares of the capital, out into the waters of the gulf. And with a mighty swirl of endless brown bodies, the army of the King turned south.

From bays and inlets and harbors, on down the coast, other bands and companies swept out to join them. From every inlet along the coast they came, summoned by the scouts of the King.

Tommy Cod moved with such speed and excitement that, without the noble golden body of the King beside him, he might soon have faltered from exhaustion. But pride made him strong—pride and faith.

And it may have been Tommy Cod himself who first sighted the great mass of the herring school. "Look! Look!" he shouted.

Off shore, in the sea ahead a million tiny gray-green bodies were traveling, filling the sea as far as the eye could reach. The King dispatched officers to induce the herring school to move closer inshore so that his cod army could protect their seaward flank.

Then Tommy Cod looked and began to tremble inside.

The invaders!

Far out in the sea beyond, coming swiftly onward toward the herring, appeared a company of dark gray shark-like bodies, stealing on through the depths like phantoms. The dogfish!

They maneuvered to cut off a great segment of herring from the main school and went in among them, turning, swirling, threshing, driving the confused and terrified mass to one side. The sea became a boiling turmoil.

Then, without warning, a detachment of cod, the wild, dark-skinned fighters from the north, flew out

[107

and struck furiously, singling out the marauders, engaging them, fighting with a frenzy such as the terrified Tommy had never dreamed of. Slashing and gnashing, they drove the invaders back and the huddled mass of terrified herring sped to rejoin the main school.

On down the coast surged the great herring school, the cod army protecting their sides and rear.

But in a few minutes the invaders returned with reinforcements. Tommy watched them coming on, slinky gray bodies winding along swiftly, glittering green eyes studding the sea like stars. Now the battle began in earnest all along the front.

It was then that Tommy became conscious of a pattern in the movements, an organized plan on the part of the King. Slowly but surely, the cod army was surrounding the army of the invaders. The army of the dogfish knew it and were battling furiously, and where they fought, hundreds of torn and bleeding warriors dropped out of the conflict to float motionless to the surface. The water was turning a murky red.

Suddenly there was a great new movement. Straight down from the waters of the north a company of seals came streaming, shooting along toward the battle area, like dark brown streaks. Once in the fray, they fought furiously to complete the circle that the cod army was

throwing around the army of the dogfish. And furiously the dogfish were fighting to break through. But the seals were flashing everywhere—all about the outskirts, snapping and slashing and racing after strays.

The great mass of the dogfish, still fighting desperately, was surrounded—a thick ring of cod was about them on all sides. And behind the cod moved the vigilant patrol of the seals. For the first time Tommy Cod saw Ho-Happy among them, and was sure of victory!

But now that they had the dogfish surrounded, what were they going to do with them? The cod army could not annihilate them—the dogfish were too numerous, too fierce.

Tommy Cod might have known that the King would have a plan for this, too. Now he could see what was happening. The surrounded dogfish army was being forced slowly, but surely, down shore.

Great Island and Lost Ship Reach were just ahead, with the tide racing through that channel between the islands and the coast. And at the outer end of the channel—Tommy shuddered. The dogfish army was being forced along inshore, along into that tide-racing channel, on toward *Spinner the Whirlpool!*

Evidently the dogfish sensed the maneuver. Fighting madly, they broke a great gap in the ring of sur-

110]

rounding cod, and were trying to escape.

For a moment it looked as if they would succeed. And then from off beyond, like a wavering pink cloud in the sea, came a mighty school of squid. A thousand pink bodies lined up before the escaping dogfish, and like a sudden thunderclap, turned all the sea in front of them inky-black. The fugitives, blinded and confused, dashed back into their close-packed army again, but the army of the squid followed. And with them went the black all-enveloping cloud.

Now the dogfish had the shore on one side of them, and the inky black water with cod and seals behind it on the other. The King summoned that company of wild northerners, massed them behind the still-fighting dogfish, and drove the enemy into the channel between shore and island—drove them into the tide running through the channel like a mill-race—the tide that began sweeping them on toward Old Spinner the Whirlpool.

From his position beside the King, Tommy Cod could hear Old Spinner roaring faintly at the other end of the channel. He saw the mass of the dogfish drawn forward in the current—swift and swifter— helpless now, being swept on—and on—into the roaring, spinning vortex.

It seemed to Tommy that the sound of Old Spinner's

[111

roaring grew heavier for a moment—thicker—duller. There was a tense, watchful space—and then, beside Tommy Cod, the King was giving sharp triumphant orders. "Attention! Assemble! Victory is ours! On to Shelter Cove!"

It was late afternoon. The slanting light of the sun's rays lit up the sandy bottom of Shelter Cove until it gleamed like gold. The rockweed and kelp shone bronze and purple; the fish loitered about idly. A wandering little school of coral-pink shrimp had drifted in from nowhere and were moving about through the clear green water like tiny pink sparks. Shelter Cove had never been so beautiful.

Grouty the Crab was the only briskly active bit of life in all the lazy afternoon. Grouty was cleaning up around his doorstone, and giving tart orders to his small crab brood.

"I want you to keep away from this doorstone with your messes," he cried out crossly to the mischievous little throng of young crabs. "If you youngsters want to have a picnic off an old dead flounder, you have it somewhere else without leaving a mess around here." He glanced sourly at a bull-headed lamper-eel lying still on the bottom watching out for scraps. "We've got scavengers and cheap trash around here as it is."

A moment later, Grouty looked up into the water above him. "Well, what do *you* want?"

A brilliant red perch had dropped down from the upper water in wide hurrying spirals, to stop in front of Grouty. "Oh, Grouty," he panted. "The greatest thing in the world has happened."

"Well, tell us about it, and don't stay there gasping."

"Some of the fish from outside have raced in—and they say that King Cod with the biggest army in all the ocean is lying outside."

"What?" snapped Grouty. "Go on! Go on!"

"And he's preparing to come on into Shelter Cove, with a big retinue—wild soldiers and all—and you'd never guess who else—Tommy Cod!"

Almost before the perch had finished telling the great news, it was relayed up and down the coast, and

114]

almost immediately the fish-folk were assembling— the sleek haddock, the harbor pollock, the perch. Down below, the bottom was alive with flat flounders, with bull-headed sculpins—horns back, wriggling hurriedly along to find the best place to watch. And strangers flocked into the cove—striped-back mackerel, lump fish and lamper-eels. Grandfather Lobster was laboriously climbing up the mounds of rockweed for a better view. The young crabs were wild with excitement.

Grouty squatted in front of his house in the rocks, scarcely moving, thinking his thoughts. And it was there that a spruce young lieutenant cod found him.

All Shelter Cove watched as the dapper young messenger saluted Grouty, and all Shelter Cove listened as he said: "King Cod sends his respects, sir, and wishes me to say that he is coming to visit Shelter Cove before sundown. With him he is bringing young Tommy Cod."

Grouty could hardly hear the rest.

"And to you, sir," the messenger was saying, "he will bring his earnest thanks and gratitude in person." The messenger saluted and swam on.

Grouty sat still, trying to look unconcerned before all the peering eyes of Shelter Cove. But when he moved out into the open where he could catch the first glimpse of King Cod and Tommy, his big front claws wobbled

[115

a bit uncertainly and his legs trembled.

And then they came—a cavalcade of honor the like of which no sea-creature on all the coast had ever seen. The waters of Shelter Cove shimmered with their splendor.

At the head of the great procession moved King Cod —a magnificent commanding presence, the light glancing and glimmering from off his splendid body. Beside him, Tommy Cod did his best to move regally like the King, but he had to wriggle along hurriedly at times, and flap his tail sharply in order to keep up. He was trying to look sober and dignified and royally un-moved, when all the time he wanted to cut loose and frolic with the youngsters he knew, and dart on ahead to see Grouty Crab.

Following him on either side was the King's guard, and behind them, a detachment of the main army—in a seemingly endless procession of gorgeous color.

First came the wild Northern Cod in their battle-scarred gold-brown coats; next the paler Banks Cod— blond creatures, almost creamy yellow. In the middle of the procession, escorted with honor, moved a detach-ment of Squids, their soft pink skins gleaming like velvet in the light; and then came a company of Seals, with the regular cod-army bringing up the rear.

On they came in a splendid moving pageant. And
116]

all the young fish of Shelter Cove swam along beside them, hurrying, shoving, sliding over each other in their excitement. The procession deployed itself around the cove, and the King, with his attendants and Tommy Cod, moved in toward the shore and came to rest before the little rock house of Grouty the Crab.

The King spoke gravely.

"Grouty Crab," he said, "I salute you—for your wisdom, for your cleverness, for your fealty. You have been of great value in your instruction to young Tommy Cod. He is the most promising of all my sons."

Grouty, enormously proud, glanced at Tommy. "Tommy Cod has inherited much from his great sire, Your Majesty. But," with a sly return to groutiness, "I suppose, after all this, there'll be no living with him in Shelter Cove."

"Not so," said the King. "I shall have him understand that true greatness is founded on humility, and that a worthy king must be a humble king."

Grouty bowed his little squat body, and the King continued.

"You have wisdom, Grouty Crab. It was clever of you to urge Tommy to search for me. For the hosts of the dogfish have been overcome and destroyed. Even now the sardine-herring are returning in peace and security all along these coasts. Shelter Cove is saved!"

[117

Grouty sat, motionless, his big arm-claws folded humbly, his legs trembling a little. He could not speak.

The King went on: "With great confidence I leave my son, Tommy Cod, with you. Through the next stage of his life guide him wisely against the day when he, himself, may be King of all the Cod."

What a great celebration followed in Shelter Cove! Tommy Cod never forgot it—the crowds, the cheering, the wonder—the coming and going—the excitement and the confusion of victory.

Later that day, in a little seaweed-hung niche in the rocks, Tommy listened to the King's parting words.

"As the son of the King you have a great opportunity before you. You have already shown that you have courage and bravery, cleverness and kindness.

But these alone are not enough. You must also possess wisdom—wisdom to use all these other qualities with justice, with mercy, with honor. You must acquire knowledge of all the seas so that you may meet and know the fish-folk of all the ocean, know the good from the bad, the friends from the enemies."

There was a little silence. Dusk was closing throughout the water and the golden presence of the King seemed to manifest itself now chiefly in his voice.

"In a year you will be almost full-grown. In a year—come again to me."

As the King and his attendants moved out to sea, the water suddenly began to shine, as though lighted by millions of fireflies.

In the wavering flashes of silver light, the King's body and those of his attendants seemed to glide away in ripples of liquid fire.

Proud and happy, Tommy Cod watched until they vanished in the dim gray mystery of the sea.

*   *   *

Vanishing . . . Vanishing . . .

Binky Seaworth roused himself. The fog was clearing. He stared up through a great rent in the mists— straight into the bright blue sky.

He reached for his oars excitedly, and pulling with all his might, started back for Shelter Cove.

For the very first time Binky cleared that great log like a bird, slipped a bit, but scrambled on. He was bursting with joy.

"It's all right!" he shouted to the men on the beach. "Everything's all right! Everything's all right!"

"What's all right now, kid?"

"Everything!" Binky repeated. "The herring will be back again!" He forgot that it was all a daydream, and went on, excitedly: "The cod and the seals and the squid licked them in the battle—and drove 'em spang into the whirlpool. Oh, it was terrible! And—"

"Binky!" Uncle Eben had come out from the shed.

"Where on earth have you been all day? Everyone's been worried." He towered over the small boy. "Now you stop talkin' all that nonsense, or I'll give you a taste of a rope's end. Now, *mind!* Go home and git your grub."

"But, Uncle Eben, I can't—I can't eat, I'm so happy. You've *got* to believe me, Uncle Eben," he pleaded earnestly. "The herring will be back—"

"Nonsense. Now you do as I say."

"But it's true! P'rhaps they'll be showing up on these shores this very day. It was an awful battle, Uncle Eben, and it was the seals and the squid that helped the King to win. And so Shelter Cove is saved and the men won't have to move away, and . . ."

Uncle Eben was pointing up the beach. "You march home like I tell you. If I hear any more of this non-sense . . ."

"If I was you," one of the men interrupted, "I'd take this kid somewhere to see a doctor. He ain't right in his head with all this stuff."

Binky straightened up on his stubby little crutch. "I *am* right, I tell you."

"Mebbe you are, son." The man's voice was gentler. "But we aint takin' any chances. Most of us are movin' on out of Shelter Cove—some of us this very day." He pointed back from the shore to little old automobiles piled high with luggage.

Binky stood forlornly. "Won't you wait—just a little while?"

Uncle Eben was ordering him again. "Home with you, now. March!"

Slowly, drearily, up the beach, he limped. Across the marsh—suddenly he stopped and wheeled about. A great shouting had risen behind him.

Far out on the water a fishing boat had rounded a point and was heading into the cove, her motor echoing loudly from off the rocks, her boatman shouting excitedly.

Binky turned, swinging himself as fast as he could down toward the shore again.

The men stood watching the boat speeding in. The boatman was waving his arm and shouting exultantly.

"Herrin' have struck!"

The men stood in silence, their faces tense—afraid to believe.

The boatman shut down his engine. He nosed in to the beach. "It's true," he cried out. "Herrin' have struck back." His face was red and shining. "Three or four of the sardine weirs had good catches in them this fore-noon." He mopped his neck excitedly. "The scout boats say the water off-shore is thick with 'em. Never saw such great schools—all along the coast."

[123

One of the men, his face grave and serious, turned to the shining-eyed Binky, caught him up in powerful arms, crutch and all, swung him to his shoulder, and started up the beach. The others burst into cheers, and followed noisily.

The rest of the day, so happy he could not speak, Binky went around in a daze watching the excited fisherman going back to their boats all up and down Shelter Cove.

And then, to top everything, Mr. Ames came back, driving to the village from inland in his government coupé. A few minutes later, his heart beating excitedly, Binky sat in the little experiment station telling him all about the story he had imagined—how real it seemed.

After a thoughtful silence, Mr. Ames said gravely: "Your story isn't all imagination, Binky. Much of it shows the things you've read, of course..." He looked at the boy wonderingly. "But there's something more that none of us can explain. Not yet..."

At sundown, Binky sat alone high up on a headland at one side of the cove. He was thinking about his story, wondering if there really *could be* a fish like King Cod, a squid like Argo, a wonderful fellow like Ho-Happy the Seal. He wondered if—

Someone came out from the spruces behind him—

124]

Uncle Eben.

"Come, Binky." Uncle Eben's face was kind.

"Uncle Eben . . . do you believe now?"

"Aye, lad. The ways o' Providence are past findin' out. I believe we've all had guidance—been steered by the power no man can fathom—the same power that moves the sea—forever and always." He stopped. "When ye git ready, come down. All the shore folk are makin' a great party for ye. And the men—all the men say that with a good season, they want t' send ye away t' school—where ye'll be taught all the things ye should know to be a great help to the fishin' industry. Yer friend, Mr. Ames, is at the head of it. I guess he knows what's what, after all."

Binky beamed. He stayed behind a moment more, looking far out to the sea, then he held up a small hand above his stubby crutch.

"Good-bye," he said. "Good-bye Grouty, and Young Cod, and Argo, and Ho-Happy the Seal. And thanks— thanks a lot."

He swung along down to the wharf where torches were flaring and fires lighted all along the shore.

He cleared the big log again without any trouble.

Binky had never been so happy.

DATE DUE